DONN BYRNE

"IRISH" & A MAN'S GAME

Adapted by:
Jerome Tiller

Illustrated by:
Liam O'Neil

Adapted Classics for Middle School
An imprint of ArtWrite Productions
1555 Gardena Ave NE
Minneapolis, MN 55432-5848

Book Design by ArtWrite Productions
Cover Design by Liam O'Neil
Edited by Davy Leitner

ISBN 978-1-939846-38-9

ILLUSTRATED
LITERATURE
FOR YOUNGSTERS
(AND OLDSTERS)

adaptedclassics.com

artwriteproductions.com

PREFACE

You are about to read adapted versions of two stories by Donn Byrne, a great, largely unappreciated author. Some changes (paragraph breaks, rearrangements, minor additions, omissions, etc.) were made to accommodate the illustration of characters and critical scenes in the story and a few to hasten the pace. Some changes (word choice, word order, minor additions, etc.) were made to expand its accessibility and appeal, keeping modern youth in mind. No change was made with the notion it would improve the text or the story.

Among other places, the original version of each story can be found at: http://www.gutenberg.org/

The *Adapted Classics* Collection

Contemporary-classic illustrations in *Adapted Classics* books add expression to visually-rich stories by world-famous authors. Lightly modified and illustrated to suit and attract modern young readers, stories in the *Adapted Classics* collection are respectful renditions of timeless stories from the world of classic literature.

View the entire collection at: www.adaptedclassics.com

Dedicated to Davy Leitner
My nephew, my friend &
true boxing enthusiast

"IRISH"

The old man sat in the doorway of one of the little houses, fronted with a yellowish patch of grass and surrounded by a warped iron railing. He hated the street with the dull, cold hatred of old men. Yet he couldn't get away from it. Often his son had suggested, and his wife had also when she was alive, that they move to the country. He would hear none of that. The son had spoken of the pleasant places in Brooklyn, out Flatbush way. What impression he had of that worthy borough is hard to imagine, but he spoke of it with devastating contempt.

The truth was, the old man was wedded to Twenty-fourth Street. He was like some men who have ancient, unattractive wives whom they despise and hate but without whom they cannot live.

Here was the place it was fated for him to be. Here was the shop where he got shaved every morning. Here was the saloon where he had his three drinks a day, regular as the clock—one before lunch, one before dinner, and one before he went to bed. Here was the news-stand where he snapped the daily paper from the hands of the old German woman. If an elevated train on Seventh Avenue were late, he would notice it. He had decided to be here, and here he remained.

Mr. Dennis McCann lived on Twenty-fourth Street in the great city of New York, and his social standing there was something of a phenomenon. Every one accorded him a sort of a terrified respect. To the eye, he was a cold figure. It was this quality, not his years, that made him old. He could not have been much over fifty. He was not a big man, but he gave the impression of size, of importance. His hair was gray, and that gave him dignity. His eye was of a colorless, aloof blue, the blue of ice. His face was gaunt, always clean-shaven. His clothes were always a decent and expensive black, and a heavy gold watch-chain spanned his vest. He had always a stick by his side. His shoes were good and roomy, and somewhat old-fashioned.

The Italian coal-and-wood man, the German newsdealer, the man in the cigar store, the bartender who fixed his drinks, the entire street where he lived and did his business recognized he was of them, but immensely superior. He was not a gentleman, so the respect was not from below to above, but something much more real. None ever became familiar with him, nor would any sane man think of insulting him. He moved through the street aloof and stern, with terrible dignity. Even the children hushed as he drew near.

None in the street ever examined their hearts or minds as to why he was paid their tribute of respect. If they had, they would have found no reason for it. But they would have paid it to him all the same. He was Mr. McCann.

And this was all the more strange because he was the father of Irish Mike McCann, the fighter who had only two men standing between himself and the middle-weight boxing championship of the world! Oh, did the street love Irish! The street was proud of him. Nonetheless, it was to the 'father of Irish', Mr. Dennis McCann himself, that *respect* was due and delivered, no strings attached.

A very strange thing about Mr. McCann was this: he could only know time and space and circumstances in relation to himself. Nothing besides his own existence mattered to him—not holidays, the changing seasons, baseball, or world events. None of these mattered in the least, and he did not bother to try to see any such things clearly.

But he could see himself in his boyhood on the Irish hills, among the plain farmer family into which he was born. He could place his father, plain old tiller of the soil, always smoking a clay pipe; his mother, warm-hearted, bustling, a great one for baking bread; his brothers and sisters, honest clods. But he himself seemed to have been born superior, was superior. There was no mystery. It was a fact. He accepted it.

And from him, his mother accepted it, and she impressed on the whole family that their son and brother Dennis was superior. For him better clothes, easier work, and when he decided that farm life was not for him, no objection was made to sending of him to college in Cork. But after a couple of years there he had made no progress with studies, and it seemed to him that the studies were not worthwhile. And he returned home.

They had tried to get a government office for him then, a very small one. But that also required examinations, which he did not seem able to pass. Thus a great contempt for books arose within him. Soon he also grew convinced that Ireland had not enough opportunity for him, so the family got the money to send him to America.

The years at the college in Cork had intensified his sense of superiority so that when he came to America he felt that the Irish he met there were a very inferior people. Yet nothing about the city pleased him either; everything was much better in Ireland, he decided, and he said Ireland was a wonderful country—the only thing wrong with it was the people. And the queer thing about it was that the Irish in New York agreed with his appraisal. His few years at Cork gave them the impression he had accumulated learning, and the Irish, common or otherwise, have a medieval respect for books and writing.

"True for you, Mr. McCann, true for you," they would say in answer to his remarks on the inferiority of the Irish who lived in Ireland. "But what can you expect considering the centuries of oppression they have been under?"

"If they had been independent enough, with just a dose of self-respect, there would not have been oppression."

"Ay, there's a lot in what you say, Mr. McCann."

His superiority disarmed them, cowed them. If one of themselves, or a foreigner, had uttered the words he spoke, I can imagine the rush to confront that person, and the dull thud, and the mournful procession to the widow's house.

His aloofness, his superiority helped him, or, rather, made him successful in the business he had chosen—life-insurance. The wisdom he uttered about life and death to Irish gents who consider life to be nothing but the lead-up to eternity impressed his hearers. So they were afraid not to take out insurance policies from this superior, young man in the know.

His superiority also brought him a wife—a timid,

warm-hearted girl who brought along to the marriage a tidy sum of money, most of which he spent upon himself. She was terrified of him and very much in love with him for years. Then the love went and the terror remained. She bore him three children, two sons and a daughter. In due time she died, but not until she had made life run pleasantly and respectfully for her husband. One son had died before her, and a short while later, the daughter, Moyra, ran away, entering a very inferior marriage with a brakeman on the Pennsylvania Railroad. One son, Mike, remained.

The time came when the old man had to retire from the field of insurance. New methods, new companies coming in, the native-Irishmen dead from consumption and pneumonia, and the Irish-American generation that followed caring not a tinker's curse for superiority. So his kingdom vanished. Gone. Kaput.

And Poles, and French, and Italians, and the folk who came from Palestine by way of Russia, and Chinese, jostled him. All Kevin McCann had left was a great sense of superiority, a growing sense of futility, and one son, "the brilliant Irish-American middle-weight, contender for the world's championship,'Irish' Mike McCann!"

All that was needed now to crown a useful and superior life, , the old man felt, was a material reward. Money he didn't care for—he had all he wanted, along with decent clothes, a house, tobacco, his three drinks a day, and "The

Advocate," an Irish weekly he read for news about people in Cork.

He often thought, as he was reading it, how much he would like to return to Ireland and show the ignorant masses there the fruits his superior life led in hard work and wisdom had brought him. But for that he would have to show something tangible—even money would not be enough, so queer those people were.

To impress them at all he would need a title of some kind: Alderman, or Judge, or Sheriff, "the Honorable Dennis McCann," and to get that he would have needed to have gone into politics, a career that wasn't for him. To succeed at that he would have had to mix with the common people in his domain; drink with them and be hail-fellow with a crowd of the dirtiest kind of Irish. No, he could never have done that.

No, but his son might have. Why couldn't he have? He was reared here right among the commoners. Sure, he came from a superior house he did, but that would only be to his advantage. They would look up to him as well as be friends with him. And with the brains one would expect he'd have considering his father, there was no office in the land for which he couldn't be fitted. Surrogate, or mayor, or governor, even! What was there to prevent that if he'd been the sort of child he ought to have been?

And if he had been that, there would have been a

monument for the old man. There would have been a justification for his life. Not that he felt he needed any, but just to show-off. And people would have recognized how much the young one owed to the old one. Then he could have gone back to Ireland for a visit. He wouldn't have stayed there; it was a good country to come from, as he always said. But even the ignorant common people would have given him credit.

He could hear them now talking to his son: "Ah, sure, if your Honor's father would have had the chances you had, sure that it isn't only the Governor of New York he'd be, but President of America. Yep, tis easy to see where you got the brains, my lad. A chip off the old block. Dennis McCann's son, the governor of the Empire State. Well, you can thank God for your father, my boy."

There would have been an evidence for him, an evidence he was entitled to. But instead, look at the dirty trick he had played upon him. Instead of the son who would crown his gray hairs with honor, who would justify him, he was father to a common prize-fighter, a man who was not looked on with respect by any. The idol, perhaps, of the New York Irish, but of the ignorant Irish.

True, he was a good boy; he didn't drink. But neither did his father, except in reason. He was generous with his money, but, after all, what was money? And he be always smiling, always laughing. "Sonny" they called him and "Irish"! That was no way to attain dignity. Even the Italian coal-ice-and-wood man called him "Irish." The old man would like to see any one call him"Irish." They'd be getting a piece of his fist or his mind, depending.

And the boy couldn't listen to any reason. The old man had an opening for him in business up-town. A friend of his, an undertaker, a very superior man, who only did the best kind of trade. He had offered young Michael a chance. But the prize-fighter had laughed.

"In a way, I'm in that line of business myself," he said with a chuckle. "Why change?"

The old man had shaken with rage.

"Get out of my sight, you impertinent pup!"

What were they thinking of Mr. Dennis McCann in Ireland, if anything at all? Someone, of course, would write home and tell all there was to tell about the Irish in America. And if my name, a name that should be treated with respect, if it came up, some one would laugh: "Old Dennis McCann! Ah, sure, what's he, anyway? Sure, his son's only a common fighter."

He could never get away from it; was never let to get away from it. Why, even tonight now, not a half-mile away at Madison Square Garden, Michael was fighting. And a great fuss they were making about it, too. Some Italian he was fighting. And if he won, he was to get a fight with the champion. He'd probably win—he always did—and he'd beat the champion, too. And the end of it would be the honorable name dragged once more through the dirt of the newspapers. That would be the long and the short of it.

"I wonder will he forget to bring home 'The Advocate', after the fight" the old man thought. "He'd better not."

Before the bell had gone for the first round, before the referee had called them together for instructions, before even the gloves were laced on him, "Irish" knew he was a beaten man.

Below him—he could see from his corner of the ring—the great garden was packed, a yellowish gray foam of faces above the dark liquid of bodies. Above those were great oval galleries lined with faces, and here and there were little tendrils of smoke. And the red caps of attendants. And occasionally the flash of metal buttons as police and firemen hovered in the aisles.

And at the shelf around the ringside reporters with their pencils and paper, and telegraphers with their clicking instruments. The timekeeper, fingering watch and gong. In another corner of the ring the thin, gloomy referee—himself once a famous lightweight. And everywhere lights, that in a minute or so would go out, and there would be only a great blue one over the ring. And over the house was the rippling hush that at any instant would burst into a great volume of cheers; a deep roar as of gunnery.

Across the ring, in his corner, the Italian middle-weight lolled, chatting with his seconds. Irish could occasionally glimpse the olive body; the dark hair and eyes; the even, grim face, unmarked save for the marred left ear and the slight flattening of the nose.

"... between the leading contenders of the world's middle-weight championship, Nick Chip [so they had Americanized Niccolo Chiapetta] of Buffalo, and Irish Mike McCann...." and the sentence was lost in the roar of the Garden.

As he came to the center of the ring for the referee's instructions, to hear the interpretation of the rules of hitting while holding and about what was and what was not a clinch, he studied the alert, smiling Italian. Yes, Chip was far and away the best man he had ever met; too good for him, much too good. If he had only waited a year, waited six months, even; five or six months more of stiff, good fighting and he could have taken the Italian easily. A little more experience and a little more confidence if he could only have waited.

But he couldn't wait; he couldn't afford to. Neither he nor the old man could afford to.

They shook hands and returned to their corners. The whistle blew, ordering the seconds out.

"Don't box him, Irish. Stay with him. Get in close, and when you get him open, bam! See, just bam!" Old Maher, his trainer, whispered as he ducked out. "See, no fancy stuff. Just sock him. How are you feeling, Irish?"

"Fine."

"At'a baby!"

Bong-g-h! He turned and walked to the center of the ring.

The Italian had dropped into his usual unorthodox pose. His open right glove fiddling gently at the air, his left arm crooked, the glove resting against his left thigh. He moved around the ring gently, like a good woman dancer.

About him was an immense economy of movement. He seemed wide open—a mark for any boxer's left hand. But Irish knew better. The Latin would sway back from the punch and counter like lightning. The old champion was wise to lie low and not to fight this man until he was compelled to.

If he could only spar him into a corner and rush him there, taking the punches on the chance of smashing him on the ropes.... But the Italian glided around like a ghost. He might have been some sort of a phantom for shadow-boxing, except for the confident, concentrated eyes.

A minute's fiddling, shifting of position, light sparring. The creaking of the boards, the shuff-shuff-shuff of feet.

"Ah, why don't you walk in and kill him, Irish? He's only a Guappo!" came a voice from the gallery.

"Irish ain't green—he's orange,"an Italian supporter jeered. "A yella green orange picked too early off da tree, ain't ya, Irish?" .

"Irish" could wait no longer. He feinted with his left, feinted again. The left shot out, missed the jaw, came home high on the head. The right missed the ribs and crashed on the Latin's back. A punch jarred Irish on the jaw. An uppercut ripped home under his heart. At close quarters the Italian was slippery as an eel. The garden roared delight at the Irish lad's punches, but Irish knew they were not effective. And the Italian had hurt him; slightly, but hurt him.

A spar, another pawing rush; light, smart blows on the ropes. "Break! break!" the cry of the referee. Creaking of ropes and whining of boards. A patter of applause as the round came to an end. A chatter of voices as the light went up. The clicking of telegraph instruments.

"At'a boy! Keep after him," Maher greeted.

As he sat down in his corner Irish was grim. Yes, the Italian was too good for him; he had been afraid of this: that the Italian would out-general him into attacking all the time.

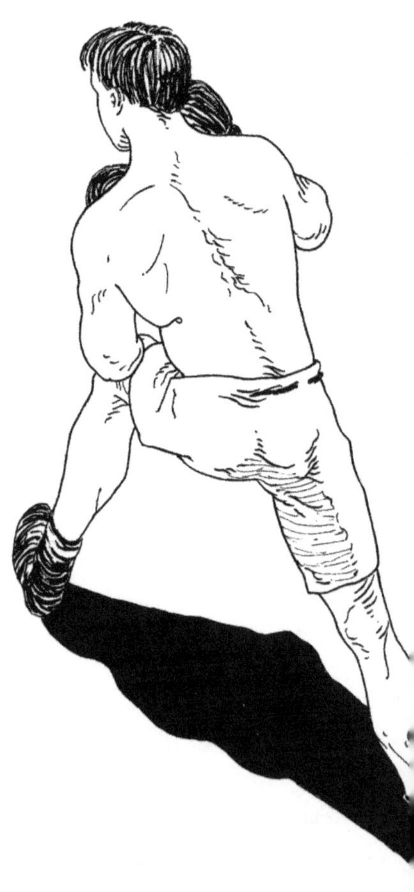

L.O.

A little more experience, the fights that mean a hundred times the theory, and he would have lain back and forced Chip to stand up and face him instead of sniping him on the run. The confidence of six or seven more fights and it wouldn't have mattered to him what the gallery was shouting, what the ringside thought. He could have made Chip stand up and fight, and in a round or so the Garden would have been with him.

If he had only had a little more experience—if only he had been able to wait!

Ah, well, what was the use of grousing! He was here to fight.

"Can't you rough him up a little in the clinch, Irish?" Maher whispered.

"No, I'll fight him fair."

"Fair? No, you gotta get his goat."

"No."

"Just a little."

"No."

The lights went out, leaving only the great glare of the ring. The whistle blew; clatter of buckets and bottles. The seconds clambered down. The gong clanged with a shuddering impact. The second round.

He walked slowly forward over the white canvas under

the bluish white arc-light, to meet his man, and then suddenly from his walk he jumped, as some jungle thing might jump. He jumped without setting, without any boxer's poise. Right for the poised, alive body he jumped. And his hands hooked for drive and uppercut. He could feel the sense of shock as they both went home, but to unvital points. The left hand thudded on the neck. The right crashed on the Italian's left arm. He was in close now, driving short lefts and rights to the body, but he was handling something that bent and sprang back like a whalebone, that moved, swayed with suppleness like some Spanish or Argentine dancer, and soon elbows locked his arms subtly, and he could do nothing.

"Come on, break!" The referee was trotting about the ring like a working terrier. Peering, moving from right to left. "Break! Break!" His voice had the peculiar whine of a dog on a scent.

He stood back, sparred a moment. Again Irish rushed. He felt on either side of his face sharp pains as of slaps with the open hand on the cheeks. Irritating things. He could feel the Latin shake as the left hand caught him flush on the ear. A tattoo like taps of little hammers played at his body. Irish's right glove came full into the Italian's ribs. He could feel the rush of air through the Italian's teeth. He brought the hand up with a short chop on the Italian's neck. A scuffle; a semi-wrestle. And again his arms were locked.

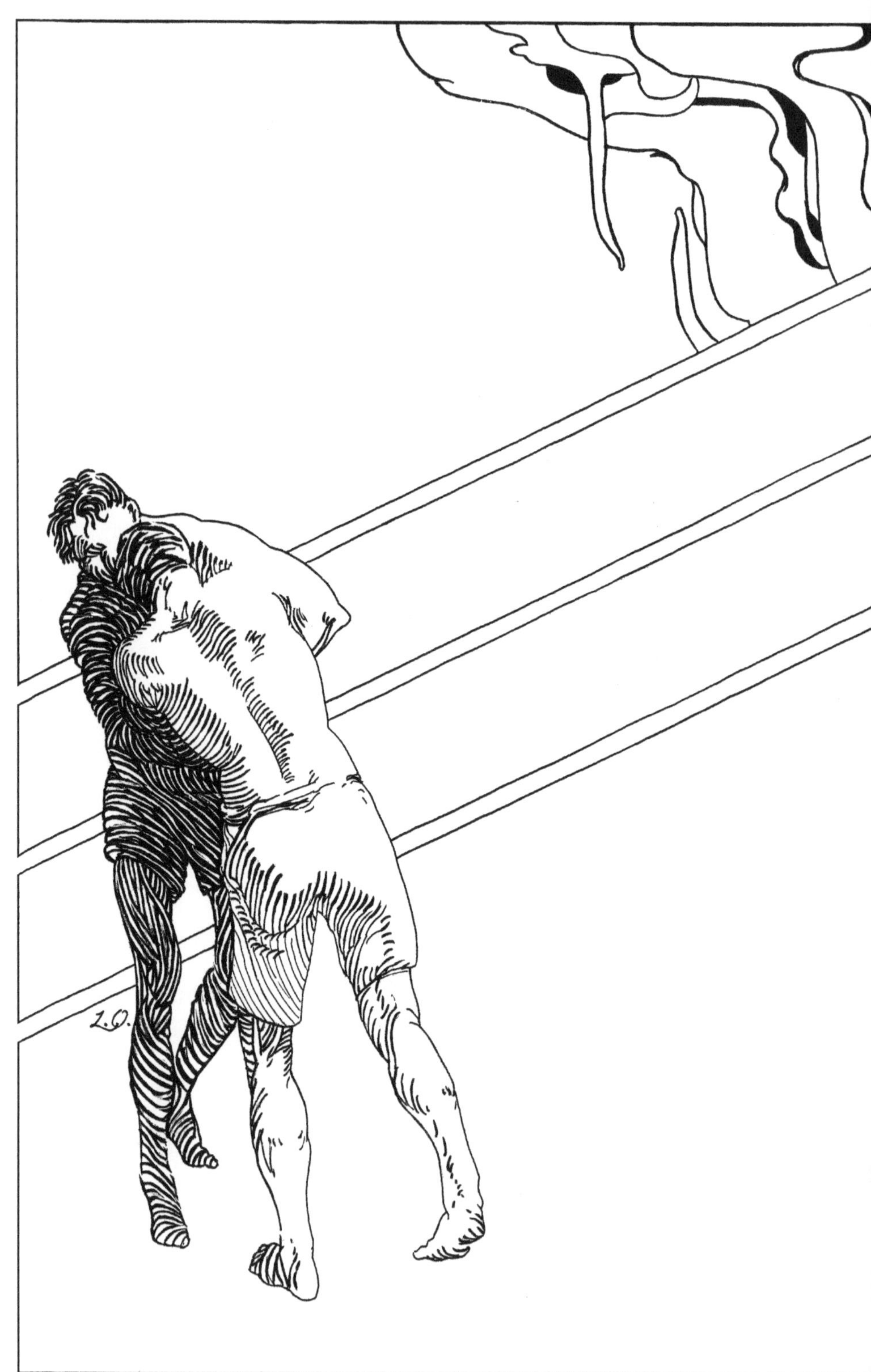

"Come on, boys! Come on! Break quick!"

They stood apart, sparred. Irish feinted with the left hand. Feinted with the right. Changed feet quickly, right foot foremost now. Pivoted home with the left hand—Joe Walcott's punch. The Italian side-stepped, and caught him on the ear as he swung to the ropes. Irish turned quickly. A flurry of gloves. Light lead and counter. Clinch.

"You're good, Nick!"

"Y'ain't so bad yourself, Irish."

As the bell finished the round and he walked toward his corner, he was surprised, looking down at himself, to find angry red welts on his body where what he thought was a light tattoo had been beaten....

Yes, he thought between rounds, given another little while, another pound of experience, that even up against Nick's cunning, his generalship, he could have beaten him. And then between himself and the championship there would have been only the champion, and the old champion's day was past. He was getting fat, and satisfied, and drinking—and that was bad! And him going around the country to Boston and New Orleans and Seattle, beating third-raters and then mainly on points, and lying low, very low indeed, whenever Nick Chip's name was mentioned, or even his name, Irish Mike McCann's. Only another six months and he could have taken on the men the champion had beaten: Paul Kennedy of Pittsburgh, and the clever Jewish lad who went by the Irish name of Al Murphy—that fight would have taught him a lot—and the Alabama Kid, the hunched Black middle-weight who hit like a flail, and Chicago Johnny Kelly—who fought with his right hand first, a hard lad to reach, but he could have beaten him. Could have beaten them all.

He wanted to be champion—knew he could be, with time and experience. And what there was for him in the championship was not personal glory and not money, but a strange pride of ease that was hard to explain. All he knew to do well was this athletic feat of fighting with gloves. There was intuition, a sort of gift. His body balanced right. His left hand moved easily. His right was always in position. All his fights he had won easily. But he had never been up against any one as good as this Italian veteran.

It seemed to him only right that an Irishman—or an Irish-American, which was better still—should hold the middle-weight and light heavy-weight championships. Fighting—clean, hard struggle—was the destiny set for them. He knew enough of the history of his race to know that. They had fought under every banner in Europe—the Irish Brigade! And Russia and Germany knew them well. Everyone knew them well, friend and foe alike. They served and fought where help and fighting was needed. Even in New York there was the beloved Sixty-ninth brigade, the Fighting Sixty-ninth, ready to go as needed. New York knew all about them, too!

Vaguely in his mind there were thoughts which he could not translate into words, it not being his craft, that there was some connection between the men who fought in a padded ring with gloves and the men who went gallantly into battle with two flags above their heads, the flag they served faithfully and the little wisp of green they loved. The men in the ring stood for the green in the field, perhaps. And we should see in the Irish boxer what the cheering ranks of Irish going into battle represented: Fight squarely in the ring, fight gallantly, fight to the last drop, and win gallantly and lose gallantly. And let no man say: There is a dirty or mean fighter. And let no man say: There is a coward.

There were Irish names in the ring that made old men's hearts flutter and young men wish they had been born years before. Old John L. Sullivan (God rest the gallant battered bones!) and Tom Sharkey of Dundalk, who never knew when he was beaten, and old Peter Maher, who was somewhere in the house. And there was another name in the mist of past days, the name of a middle-weight champion who had been greatest and most gallant of them all, the original, bare-knuckled Jack Dempsey, the 'Nonpariel', the 'Unbeatable'. None like him, none! Irish of the Irish, most gallant of them all, he sleeps in a green grave in the West somewhere, and in all men's hearts.

And Irish had thought humbly to fill the Unbeatable's shoes, to fight as hard as he fought, to win as chivalrously, to lose as well. And in his corner, as he fought, the ghost

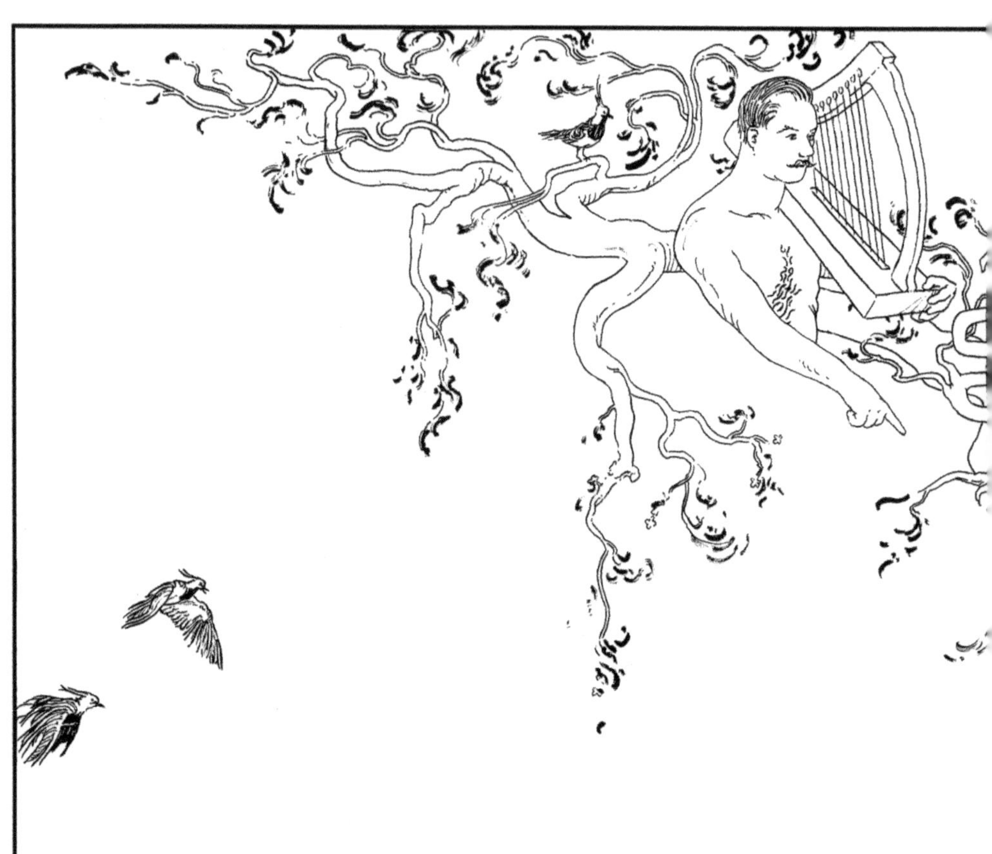

of the great Dempsey would there be. And the roar of the house as he would walk out at the referee's call, the champion, Irish-American, in his tights of green, and around his waist the starry Western flag.

Ah, well!

The shrill cut of the whistle, and the chief second leaned forward and wiped his face.

"Fift' round, Irish. Keep at him, boy!"

The gong, and the hushed house.

He noticed now that the Italian fighter was no longer resting his left hand semi-casually on his hip, kept up no longer his poise of an Argentine dancer. The Buffalo man's left hand was extended like an iron bar, his shoulder hunched to his jaw for a shield, his head sunk low, as a turtle's head is half-drawn under its shell; his feet well apart. The man's oily black hair was a tangled mop, and on his ribs were red blotches. His lips were set in a wide line. His black, snake-like eyes snapped and glowed, and his poised right hand flickered like a snake's tongue.

And he was punching, punching as hard as he could, hitting squarely with knuckles and every ounce of weight—careless of the economy of the ring that tells a man to save his hands. For a boxer's hands are a boxer's life, and every hurt sinew, every broken knuckle, every jarred delicate bone counts in the long run. The Italian was hitting, hitting like a trip-hammer, hitting for his title.

They faced each other, the Italian poised, drawn like a bowstring, aiming like a sharpshooter, Irish, jigging on his toes, careless of guarding, feinting with the right hand, breaking ground, feinting with the left, feinting with the right again, and then a sudden plunging rush. The jar to his neck as the Italian's straight left caught him flush on the mouth, the whirling crash of infighting, the wrestling clinch. No longer the referee called, "Break! break!" but tore at them with hysterical hands. A tacit understanding grew between them to protect at all times, and as they drew apart they hooked and uppercutted, Irish with an insane mood of fighting, the Italian with a quick deliberation: –Snap! Snap!–the punches.

Patter of feet, and creak of the boards, and little whine of the ropes. The great blue light overhead, the click of the telegraph instruments below. The running feet of the referee and the nervous patting of his hands, –clop! clop!– The seconds with their eyes glued on the fighting men, and their hands sparring in sympathy. The mooing roar of the crowd and their louder tense silence. And the regular gong, the short respite, hardly a second it seemed, though the interval was a minute—and the gong again.

Once they were so carried away they paid no attention to it, but fought on. Only the referee parted them. Irish held out his glove in apology and they shook hands. The garden seemed to shake to the cheering.

Whip of lead in the tenth round, crash of counter,

deep sock of infighting. Clinch; break. A half-second's inattention on the Italian's part, and the left hand of Irish crashed home to the jaw.

Himself did not understand what had happened until he noticed the crumpled figure on the boards and heard the referee:

"Get back, McCann. Get back! ... One! ... two..." An immense hysteria of sound filled the house. Men jumped on seats. The telegraph instruments clattered madly. Somewhere near the ring was a fist fight.

"Three!"

The crumpled figure twitched. At four it was dragging itself to its hands. The glazed eyes blinked. Life returned. The Italian shook his head. At seven he was on his hands and knees, his head clearing. At eight he was kneeling on one knee, one glove resting on boards. God! how long the seconds were, Irish thought.

"Nine!" Slowly the Italian rose.

The Garden was no longer filled with human beings but with instruments of baritone sound. It hit the roof, rebounded, whirled, surged. All about Irish was sound, sound. In front of him the Italian weak at the knees. The referee hunched like a bowler. Irish jumped in, fists swinging. His fists met crossed arms, elbows, shoulders, but not jaw or head. And suddenly the Italian was clinging to him, as a terrified cat will cling—he couldn't tear himself loose. It took the referee and him to tear the Italian away.

Insane with the din, blind with excitement, he rushed again to meet the beautiful diagonal coverup, left arm across heart and plexus, right crooked about throat and jaw. Again the clinging of the cat. And he felt the Italian growing stronger. It was like a dead man coming to life again. Life was flowing slowly back to shoulders, from shoulders to arms and hands, to hips and knees.

He stood back to consider this miracle, to think what to do next. Two shaking lefts caught him in the face.

And the gong rang and his chance was gone.

Yes another six months and he could have won. He would have known how to keep his head, how to finish the Italian crisply. He had him out, out clean. Another punch would have finished it. And he hadn't experience enough—another six months.

Well, what was the use of grousing! It couldn't be helped. He couldn't pass the fight up when it was offered to him. Right at home, and so much money.

The money had been needed for the home and the old man. It was funny how much a home cost even on Twenty-fourth Street, and the old man was used to a certain way of living. He liked to have a cook, and a girl to do the work around the house. That was the way it was in Ireland. And the old man needed his decent clothes and his spending money for his little drink and his tobacco and papers, and things like that. He couldn't very well put the old man in lodgings. He wasn't accustomed to that. He wanted his home and the cook and girl. He always was accustomed to it, and why shouldn't he have it?

But a house took an awful lot of money. For what the house cost he and the old man could have stayed at a swell hotel. But the old man liked to be by himself. You couldn't blame him; the old man was entitled to a home. He was a queer, crusty sort, the old man. No harm in him, you know, but just couldn't get on.

And for all that people thought, a boxer's money wasn't easy. A middle-weight didn't get the money light-weights and heavy-weights got. If he'd won the championship—ah, that was all right! Let it go! But when you split fifty-fifty with your manager, there was only half of what you fought for; and there was expenses, too. You had to travel a lot, and be nice to people, too. You had to spend a lot in saloons, though you never drank yourself. Keep your end up with the crowd. And there was always old fighters out of luck, and some of them had families, too. You couldn't refuse them even if you'd wanted to. And who's going to help out a fighter except a fighter? And there was always a lot of poor folks.

It seemed a pity, even for the money end, not to have waited. If he'd waited he'd have had the championship, and then he'd have been fixed for life.

If his old man had been a different kind of old man he'd have gone to him and said: "Hey, old timer, how about going easy on the jack for a while, hey? Just lay off a bit until I get things right. Give me another half-dozen fights under my belt, see, and I'll drop this palooka cold. And then the champion will have to give me a fight—the papers will make him, and you know what he is. He's a bum. So what do you say we get us a couple o' rooms, hey, and go easy for a while? What do you say?"

A different kind of old man would have said: "Sure. We'll take our time, and we'll knock this greaser for a row of jam-jars. And as for the champion, it's a cinch."

But he wasn't that kind of old man. He didn't hold with this fighting, nohow. He had no use for it. And he wasn't the kind of old guy you could talk to. Irish thought his pa must have had a hard time in his life.

Ah, well; he was entitled to a good time now. Let him have his own way. Irish could always make money. It didn't matter so much, after all, did it? The only thing that hurt him was that he would never draw the Stars and Stripes through the green Irish tights....

And he could have, if he'd had only six months.

Irish was aware now as he answered the bell that his bolt was shot. The high pitch of concentration had gone. With the dropping of the Italian, and the Italian's escape, he had reached the high point of his fighting, and now must go down. His punch would be heavy still, but it would lack the terrific speed, the speed of shock, that carries a knock-out.

And the effect of the cumulation of blows from the Italian sharpshooter was beginning to tell. Through the bruises on his body and neck and the puffiness of his face, energy was flowing out of him like water from some pierced vessel. The stinging lefts to his face had made it hard for him to breathe, and his hands were swollen inside his gloves, and all of a sudden his legs were tired.

Into ten rounds of whirlwind fighting he had foolishly put everything, gambled energy and hands and brain.

And he sensed with a great sinking of his heart that Chip was drawing ahead of him now, drawing away from him in the contest, with the inevitableness of the winner drawing away from the beaten man, forging ahead while the other plods hopelessly on....

With the quick telepathy of the ring the Italian knew Irish had cracked, that he was gone. And now the energy he had saved by making his man come to him he could use, he must use. For that knock-down in the tenth was a high score of points against him. And he was afraid of a draw. He would have to fight Irish again. Not again! He must knock him out.

The Italian met futile rushes with stinging lefts. At close quarters he ripped home his hands mercilessly. As they drew apart he stalked his man. Smack! Smack! It was no hard matter to avoid the rushing of Irish. God! What a glutton Irish was! What he could take without going down!

Mechanically, stolidly, dully, Irish boxed. All about him now was the hoarse murmur of speculation, and the din of it dazed him a little, and the light. And from a cut in his forehead the blood was running into his eyes.

Four times the gong crashed, the end and opening of a round, and the end and opening of another round. Dully he went to his corner. The splash of water in his face did not revive him, nor the current from the whipping towels, nor the slapping of his legs.

"Don't let him knock you out, Irish. Hold him. Only two more rounds. Don't let him knock you out." Maher's fierce whisper hit at his ear-drums. So it was as bad as that, hey?

"Hold on to him, kid. Don't fight him. Hold him."

The bell rang. They pushed him to his seat. Wearily he moved toward the center of the ring.

"Look out!" some one called.

The Italian had sprung from his corner with the spring of a cat. And Irish felt surprised that he had been struck with two terrific hammers on the jaw. And as he wondered who had hit him his knees buckled surprisingly, and he was on his hands and knees on the floor.

And he heard some one say: "... three ... four..." He struggled to his feet. Somewhere Maher was shouting. "Take the count, Irish." Irish dully wondered what he meant.

And now Chip was in front of him, concentrated, poised. And once more the hammer crashed on the jaw. And he tumbled to the boards on his side.

He was very dull, very dazed. For a while he knew nothing. And then he understood; the referee pumping his hand up and down, and the roar of the crowd.

"Eight!"

As he moved he felt the ropes, and blindly he groped for them, pulling himself to his feet somehow.

About him the din surged. The referee stepped back. The Italian was pawing at the referee's arm, protesting. Irish understood.

Chip wanted the fight stopped, didn't want to hit him any more. Ah, he was a good kid, Chip was.

And then the ring slithered underneath him; the hand grasping the rope grew lifeless, let go; and the lights went out for him; and Irish crashed forward on his face.

The old man looked at his boy's face, all battered above the blue serge suit.

"Well," he said, "it must have been a grand fight entirely!"

"It was a great fight," Irish grinned, "and a good man won."

"Meaning yourself?"

"No, meaning the Italian."

"The Dago?"

"The Italian."

"So you were beat, eh?" the old man jeered. "I never thought you were much good at it."

"Ah, I don't know." And Irish grinned again.

"Tell me," the old man snapped, "did you bring me 'The Advocate'?"

"I did." And Irish handed it over.

"'Tis a wonder you remembered it," the old man snarled. "And after taking the fine lacing you took!"

And Irish grinned again. Wasn't he a queer, grumpy old man!

L.O.

the end

A MAN'S GAME

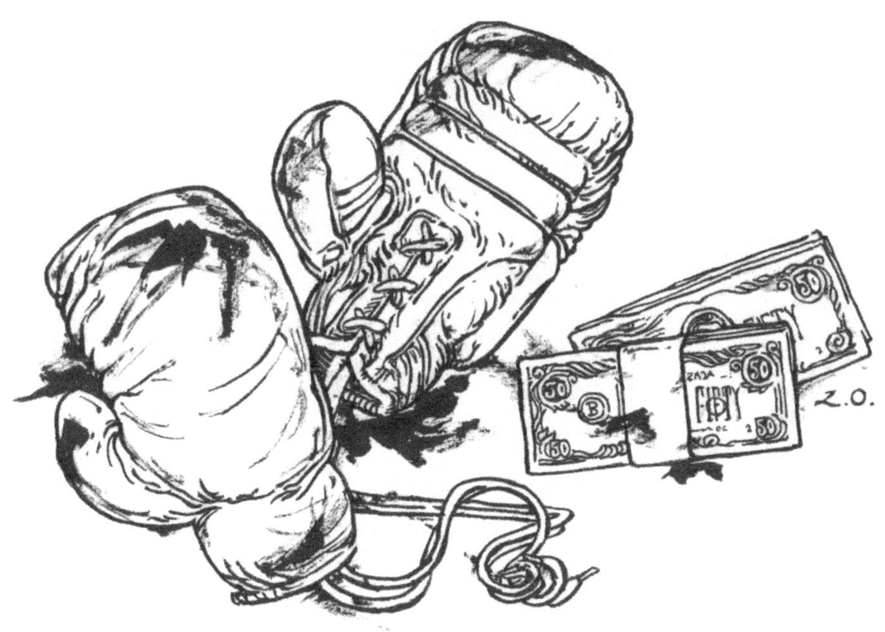

They might have kept their eight thousand dollars, Doran thought bitterly, as he went back to his corner after the first round; they might have kept their eight thousand in their pockets. If he hadn't agreed to lie down in the twelfth round, he would have been put out in the eighth. Good heavens! Couldn't they have left him at home in peace and not have brought him back to shame and humiliation tonight?

The house settled down to a humming criticism of the round. There had been nothing in it but slow, shuffling footwork, careful sparring, and a few light taps to head and chest. That was the way good fights began, they said; and this ought to be a good one, if length of time they had waited for it were anything to go by. They had seen young Nelson, the Swede, rise from preliminary to star bout, and tonight he was getting his chance at the world's championship.

But old Dan Doran—how hard it had been to get him back into action. Now here they were at last. Nelson was getting his chance at the title, and it looked as if it were going to be a corking good fight.

From his corner Doran was taking in every detail of the setting with a feeling of curious satisfaction. It was two years since he had fought, and he put out Humphreys, the slogging New Zealander, in the eighteenth round of a terrific battle. He remembered how the house had staggered to its feet at the last slashing rally, and how they had held their breaths when he had finished the fight with a smashing right cross to the jaw.

And here tonight was the same white canvas floor beneath him, stout hempen ropes about him, and good oak planking that gave in to his feet like a spring-board. And overhead was the gigantic arc light that hissed and sputtered like an engine. And on all four sides of him lay the sea of white faces stretching into the distance like blurs of linen cloth.

Old memories of forgotten fights welled up in him. There was the familiar, hoarse shouting of peanut men and lemonade boys and program sellers. There were the tense, expectant faces of the newspaper reporters and the cheery smiles of old devotees of the ring who had seen him win his title, defend it, and hold it time and time again. He felt as if he were coming home after a long journey, and that these little landmarks were recalling themselves to him and welcoming him among them again.

There was a sharp-barked order from the referee. The seconds clambered out of the ring. There was a long shudder and shuffle as the audience settled themselves back in their chairs. Clouds of blue tobacco smoke eddied and swirled toward the ceiling.The gong rang out like the bell of a church, and the second round was on.

As Doran rose and walked forward, the pleasure of the old surroundings faded off, replaced by a bitter feeling that this was his last fight and he was faking it. Old champions must go and new champions come, he knew. But this lad might have had the title for all he cared. When he put out Humphreys he had sworn it would be his last fight, but they wouldn't leave him alone on his New Jersey farm. They had to drag him out to satisfy the public that Nelson was the better man. And, not content with that, and knowing he was hard pushed for money, they had bought the honor of his ring career as a peddler buys old clothes.

They were sparring now. Doran noticed, with a tinge of envy, the huge shoulders and tapering waist of the challenger. How easily his arms moved, he thought—like a piece of well-oiled mechanism. There wasn't much brain behind the bulldog face and closely cropped forehead, but the man could move as lightly on his feet as a dancer, and there was the rosy tinge to his skin that told of youth and unspent energy and of huge reserves of strength.

He remembered the glimpse he had caught of himself when he weighed-in that morning: the bulging, knotted muscles that years in the ring had set and stiffened, the great veins standing out on his forearm that showed he was past his prime, the deep-set eyes that should have been reading a farm journal instead of probing the mind of a ring opponent, the little hollows in his cheeks, the hair beginning to grizzle and thin at the temples.

The Swede's right went out in a quick feint, and Doran dropped his head to avoid the smashing left lead that followed. There was a blow along his ribs like the stroke of a giant hammer. His right snapped home a short uppercut to the body, and they reeled to the ropes in a clinch.

He ought to have blocked that right-hander, he said to himself, with a quick flash of shame. He wasn't thinking fast enough—he was stale. They might have kept that eight thousand dollars.

The house had half risen to its feet at Nelson's rush. They had seen that before. That had finished the ring career of Sapper Murphy, and of Frank Boyd, and of Battling Hughie Madden —that vicious left drive to the jaw and right swing to the ribs. They hadn't expected to see Danny Doran go under to it, but they couldn't sit still while it was being tried. They were relieved to see Danny pushing against his man in the clinch. They settled down again. This was going to be a fight.

The referee pried the men apart, grunting with the effort. The Swede was grinning behind his guard. If he could put out the old fighter right away, why, so much more credit for him. If he couldn't, there was the agreement that the champion would lie down in the twelfth round. At any rate he was safe. The title was his.

But as he felt his right go home to the ribs true and heavy, he knew he would put out this old champion. The world's best men for seven years before him had battered the man yet left him standing while succumbing one by one to his ring generalship and craft. He would show those losers and everyone else that this fighting Swede was all that his backers were saying about him.

Doran wished he could put it all out of his head. He wanted to concentrate on the flicking, flying brown gloves in front of him. He wanted to keep his eye on the point of jaw that peeked in and out of the challenger's left shoulder, and on the challenger's ribs, and on the little knot of muscle below his breastbone. He must put up some kind of a fight even though he was to lie down.

The Swede's long left lashed out like the kick of a horse. The champion caught it on his right wrist and countered heavily on the mouth. A couple of muffled hooks and jabs at close quarters, and they were in a clinch again. The boards groaned beneath their wrestling steps, and the hemp ropes strained and creaked. There was the gruff command of the referee to break away, and the gong clanged the end of the round.

Even Dave Rogers would hardly speak to him—"Red" Dave, who had trained him for a hundred fights. He remembered every fight when Dave had knelt by his side in the corner, advising, directing, telling him the weak points of an opponent, explaining to him the secret of a guard, or how to lure his man on to the pile-driving right cross that had won him so many battles. Dave was waving a towel in front of him tonight, but there was no advice or encouragement or praise from him. He was afraid to look up and see what was in Dave's eyes.

What the devil had he ever done it for? he asked himself savagely. Why had he ever been tempted to get back in the ring? He remembered the Sunday they had crowded into the farm parlor, all big and burly and prosperous looking—Brogan, the sly theatrical man; Collier, who owned the boxing club, and Barton, the Swede's manager.

"Give the lad a square deal, Danny," they had said; "let him fight you for it. Don't let it be said you laid down your gloves and gave him the title for charity. Be a sport, Danny. You were always square. Be it now."

Besides the money he'd get for the match, that's how they got him to fight again. They appealed to his decency. And to his pride. If only he had stuck to his decision to hang up his gloves! If only he hadn't strapped them on again!!

The announcer called the third round. There was a moment's pause, and the referee ordered the seconds out. The gong broke into a reverberant trill, and the men shuffled forward to the center of the ring. There would be no action for a few rounds yet, the house agreed—they hadn't felt each other out sufficiently.

When the real fighting came, it would be a story to go down in ring history. It would be the story of the old champion, with his craft and his caution and his science, calculating time and distance to the slightest fraction, conserving every ounce of energy against this turbulent, bull-necked fighter, a thug who would throw away his strength and stamina riotously, boring and rushing and taking punishment, relying on his brute strength and punch to win.

The men shuffled around the ring in the opening spar, the old champion crouching well forward, his hands open and hardly moving; the challenger upright, his left well out, and fiddling with both gloves, as if they were operated by a set of wires. The house rose to its feet with a shout. Doran's left had snapped home clean and straight to the challenger's head, flicked out again, and driven it back between his shoulders a second time. A fierce rush from the Swede, and the champion had rushed home an uppercut to the jaw and slid into a clinch. The house roared with applause as his right glove cracked twice into the kidneys before they broke away.

L.O.

A short, rapid spar. A vision of four brown gloves cutting through the air like the lashes of whips. Light leads and counters muffled and blocked. The monotonous shuffle of the men on the resined floor. The clatter of telegraph keys reporting the round over thousands of miles of wire and cable. An ineffectual clinch or two in which the boxers swayed to and fro and the boards groaned and the ropes creaked. A grunt as a right went home, and the bell ended the third round.

That wasn't so bad, Doran thought; he could still box. The old timing and science that got and kept him his title were his yet.

“Good old Danny!” somebody shouted from the ringside. "You've got him going."

Then despondency fell on him like a pall. He had no right to praise or encouragement. He was cheating all these people. He was faking the fight. But it was for the boy that he did it. Eight thousand dollars and a chance for the boy on lower Broadway! He was gonna get the chance Danny never had. In a few years he would be through at high school, and would go up to college to study law. The meager thousands Danny had saved wouldn’t go far when there was the five years’ course to be paid for. It was this that had weighed heavy with Danny when the promoters came to lure him back to the ring for the fight. This was for his boy!

So then his training began, and it had gone very badly. The punching bag would not dance and drum under his hands as it had done two years before. His step was not so springy when he set out for the morning trot. He tired too

quickly under the medicine ball, and his sparring partners complained that his punch had not the snap and sting that had made their jobs such a hard one when he was training for Humphreys. It was then that he knew he couldn't have won anyway. He knew that. The old fire had gone.

This had weighed with him when the Swede's scout had slipped into his training quarters with a shifty glance in his eye, an evil smile on his twisted face and the offer of money. The scout had been thrown out on his head the first and second times, then Danny listened to him and threw him out again. But he couldn't win—he knew that. The old fire had gone. So Danny agreed to it. Eight thousand dollars and a chance for the boy on lower Broadway! And why, he argued to himself—and he knew he was wrong—shouldn't this young fellow pay well for the title belt if he wanted so badly to be champion of the world?

Still, though Danny doubted, his trainers had hope. It was not until the day before the match that he shamefacedly told Dave, his trainer, about the fix. But no one else.

"I never thought you'd do it, Danny," Dave had said; "I never thought it was in you."

Dave had hardly spoken two words to him in the hours since Danny spilled his rancid beans. It was only the memories of the old days when the champion fought ten rounds for five-dollar bills that brought his trainer to the ring tonight. For Danny and Dave had seen it through together for a long, long time.

The bell for round four rang, his seconds pulled the stool from under him, and he dropped into his crouch, just barely in time to avoid the challenger's thundering rush. Hook and jabs pelted home on his ribs like rain. He was giving ground. He tried to cover up and fall into a clinch. A right hook went home to his neck with a force that jarred him from head to heel. A left swing blocked, and he was holding on. The house gripped its chairs in wild excitement. This new challenger was a terror! Even Danny Doran couldn't stand punishment like this.There was a humming buzz of comment as the men broke away.

Doran felt strangely out of it. It was as if he were at a preliminary where an inexperienced novice was being cut to pieces. There was a time when he could have met a rush like that with stinging rights and lefts to the face that would have taught his man to keep his distance. A half dozen more rushes like that, he felt, and he would be out.

The Swede was sparring now, his huge bulk thrown slightly backward, his massive left arm moving in and out like the crank of a piston. His feet tapped the floor like drumsticks. His right glove, close to his ribs, suggested a coiled-up spring. His shoulders jutted backward and forward in nervous, threatening feints. He was working Doran into a corner, where he could volley down on him with another terrific rush.

L.O.

What was Doran doing? the audience wondered. He wasn't fighting, that was sure. Why, there was the Swede on him again, carrying him toward the ropes, pelting him with a shower of hooks and jabs. And Danny was covering up and looking for a clinch.

"Fight him, Danny," somebody yelled. "Wake up! You're asleep." Somewhere back in the hall a boy hooted. He tried a feeble lead as they broke away, and the bell ended the round.

He couldn't fight. Somehow he hadn't the heart in him. There was something wrong. It was as if he had come into the ring with his hands tied, to be knocked out, to have nothing to do but to lose. He was just a piece of machinery by which the Swede was to become champion of the world; just something necessary to the battle, like the panting seconds, or the timekeeper's bell.

When he entered the club that night, he had thought of his return home to the farm with a feeling of warm satisfaction. His wife would be there waiting for him, and the boy. He pictured them sitting in suspense in the parlor; his wife, big, capable, brown-haired, brown-eyed, firm-mouthed, silent; the boy lank, loosely built, red- haired, excited. How often she had waited up to welcome him back in her warm, silent way, and to dress the big blue bruises and the angry red cuts ! This would be the first time he had come home beaten in ten years. There would be a warmer welcome for him than if he had won, but the boy would be brokenhearted. Yet, the price of his championship would be in his pocket, and the price of the boy's chance. At home, they didn't know.

Z.O.

He wasn't so sure of the satisfaction now. He felt he would be more ashamed to meet their glances than to meet the eyes of Dave. If ever they got to know about it—Good God! If ever they got to know about it!

He felt a wave of heartsickness sweep over him as he got up for the fifth round. His pink-skinned, swaying opponent took on the aspect of an executioner about to mete out justice to his criminal self. The roped ring reminded him of a picture he once saw of the gallows of a guillotine. The timekeeper and the referee were presiding officers of the law. The tense, white-faced audience were citizens come to see justice consummated.

His head was rocked backward and sideways with long-range, welting swings. A mass of pulsing, irresistible rock bore down on him. His neck and sides seemed to quiver under the strokes of a jackhammer. Unspeakably racking blows smashed home to his jaw and head. People were shouting in an immense, swelling volume of sound. The floor of the ring swayed like the deck of a boat; the flaming, flashing arc light became a lone star in a black sky. He was plunging forward into dark space and then grasping and holding onto something as a swimmer grips a piece of driftwood. Consciousness came back to him little by little, and he noticed, in a dull, surprised way, that he was holding his man off by long left jabs and mechanical footwork. The bell rang in a faint, distant murmur, and he staggered toward his seconds.

The crowd was strangely silent. A sort of heavy gloom seemed to have fallen over them. They were seeing a champion passing; they were witnesses at the beating of the old ring general who for ten years had beaten the best men the world could produce. There was something terribly big about it, something infinitely pathetic.

"Poor old Danny!" he heard some one at the ringside say. "He's done for."

The flap of the waving towels rang out like gunshots. He could feel the cold comfort of the sponge passing over his face, and the slice of lemon between his lips. Somehow he felt that the crowd were sorry for him, that their sympathy had passed from the turbulent Swede adventuring for a championship to the tired old boxer defending it. If they knew what he was doing they would hail him with hisses and catcalls and execrations; they would have nothing for him but anger and contempt.

Back in the hall he could hear the hoarse, monotonous chant of the bookmakers:

"Two to one against Doran! We'll give two to one against Doran! Two to one! Two to one! Two to one!"

A wild panic seized him. People were betting on him—old ring followers, boxers, and sportsmen. He felt suddenly like a thief. He wanted to get up and shout to them that they were losing their money. He couldn't win. It was as much as he could do to last to the twelfth round for the price of his championship.

There was a commotion behind him. He heard a faint cheer and a volley of hand-clapping. Davy, the trainer, looked away. He heard his name called :·

"Hey, Danny! Danny Doran!"

He looked down. Peering up at him from the corner, he saw a broad, tanned face, with a broad, kindly mouth, shrewd blue eyes, and a nose slightly twisted to one side. There was a closely cropped head that was going bald and gray at the temples. There were two ears battered out of recognition.

"What's wrong with you, Danny, man? What's happened to you tonight?"

Doran could hardly believe his eyes. It was Tom Squires, Tom Squires from whom he had won the title ten years ago—"Honest Tom Squires" they called him then. It was like seeing someone from a dead world. Why, Tom had disappeared five years ago, no one knew where. They said he was down and out, that he had no money, that he was earning a few dollars coaching schoolboys.

"Here, let me up in that corner! Hold this coat, will you? "

Danny saw him clamber into the ring. There was something uncanny about him. It was like a ghost walking into a warm, lighted room. Danny saw him take the sponge and smelling salts from a white-sweatered second, and bend over him. The house was roaring itself hoarse with excitement.

Some of the older patrons had seen Squires lurch, reel, catch the ropes, and slip to the canvas in the thirty-fifth round against Doran more than ten years ago. By God! they said to themselves; there were fighters in those days; they were no vaudeville boxers.

Danny could hear the old fighter purring away as he held the salts to his nose :

" Why, Danny, you ought to put him out in a round. Get into it! Show them how we used to box. I came a hundred miles to see you fight tonight. Wait a minute! I was forgetting something. I want to do a little betting."

He dug his left hand into his trousers pocket. A roll of small bills came out. Danny could see that they were pitifully few. There could hardly have been more than fifteen dollars there; perhaps not that much. Squires turned to a second.

"Put that on Danny for me," he said, "and see that you get good odds, young fellow!"

The gong clanged out, clamorous, vibrant, imperious. Doran saw the huge bulk of the challenger rise slowly from his stool. He felt Squires slap him smartly on the shoulder.

"Go win, old champion," he was saying."Go in and win."

The house thundered applause as Doran rose.

He saw figures rising at the ringside and cheering wildly. There were men he recognized, old backers, old fighters, old followers of the ring. There were Colonel Knox, who had helped him when the boy was born, and Jim Mann, who had backed him against The Kangaroo, and Gentleman John Brady, whose ring career he had finished seven years before, and Tony Lavigne and Cyclone Kenny, and other old forgotten faces. They were cheering the rafters off the club.

The Swede feinted with the left glove. In a moment he would feint with the right and come rushing in, swinging both hands. The right feint came. Doran braced himself and lashed out with right and left. He ducked the flailing swings, and drove a hook to the stomach.

" That's the stuff, Danny!" someone shouted. "Keep it up!"

They sparred a few moments. Doran could see two red spots on the challenger's cheek bones where the stinging hooks had caught him; he was excited and annoyed. The easy, contemptuous smile had gone from his face. There was a hard, flashing glitter in his eyes. Doran saw him bend slightly at the knees. He was getting ready to spring. The champion shot out his left.

Then again the trip hammers smashing down his guard and ripping it up from below, the thrusting of the rock-like fighting machine against body and head and jaw, the merciless crushing of the massive arms, the sharp, nervous jar of the kidney punch, a sharp blow from the Swede's shoulder to his mouth.

Z.O.

The referee slapped them on the backs. "Break away, there!" he cautioned. "Break away! Take care, Nelson; this is a boxing match, not a free for all! "

They sparred again. Doran could not get out of his head the figure of old Tom Squires clambering into his corner and the cheering, friendly faces at the ringside. There were thousands present tonight who had cheered him to victory in the old days, who were trusting him, who were laying money on him. And he was going to lie down. He felt dull and dazed.

What did they want him to do? he asked. Did they want him to win? He couldn't do that. His science and craft were nothing without the snap that sent a punch home like a rifle bullet, and the stamina that would freshen up in the minute's rest after three minutes' slogging punishment. He couldn't do anything without them, and they were gone.

The challenger's left caught him lightly on the temple, and he slid to the right in time to avoid the murderous drive to the ribs. Old Tom Squires at the ringside had brightened him up. The old tricky footwork was coming back to him. Mechanically his eye saw an opening, and mechanically his left shot out to take advantage. There were a few snappy jabs to jaw and neck, a few swings ducked, uppercuts missed and hooks muffled, and he was in his corner again.

What did they want him to do, if he couldn't win? he asked himself. He looked at Dave flapping the towel in front of him, and at Squires whispering unheeded advice into his ear, and suddenly the answer electrified him: To fight, if only to lose; to fight, as doomed defenders of a fortress fight; to fall, as soldiers on a forlorn hope fall; to go down as a champion should, fighting; to play a man's part in a man's game, and to lose like a man.

To the devil with their eight thousand dollars! To the devil with themselves for sneaking, evil-minded, trafficking thieves! He was fighting his last fight, and he'd fight it square. He would play the game, the big game, a man's game.

He motioned Dave down with his gloved right hand. The scarred, badger-like trainer leaned toward him.

"What is it, Danny? "

"I'm going to fight, Dave". He didn't know how to put it. "This lying-down business is off."

"Why is it off, Danny? Do you think you can win?" Dave's eyes were as hard and steely as before.

"No, I don't think I can win. I'm going to lose, but I'm going to lose fair."

Dave was down by his side like a flash. Squires caught his towel and began cracking it like the lash of a whip. "Get down lower!" Dave was directing. "Keep down, and he can't get you with that left swing! "

Oh, it was good, Doran felt, to have him kneeling there in the corner advising and nursing him as he had done in every fight until now.

As he rose at the bell, it seemed to him that the thousands of closely packed, dim figures in the hall were men supporting him in the fight; that Dave and Squires in the corner were lieutenants of his; that the timekeeper's bell and the sputtering arc light were standards of battle. By Heaven! He'd show him; he'd show this peddling boxer how champions lose!

The house had grown still and tense—the great fight they had expected was in full swing, the fight between the crafty old ring general and the hurtling challenger. The waxed shoes of the boxers slid over the canvas like the rustle of silk. The referee's feet pattered as he sprang aside from the feinting, shifting fighters. The staccato rattle of the telegraph keys rang out like the beating of hammers. The pulsing, hissing breath of the audience suggested the winging of birds.

Again the swinging, thundering rush. Doran struck out savagely with both hands, and covered up. They swung around the ring in a clinch. Over the Swede's shoulder, Doran could see the figures in his corner leaping with excitement. Squires was sparring viciously at an imaginary opponent, his eyes blazing, his grim, rugged jaw thrust forward. Dave was signaling to uppercut. He worked his right arm free cautiously, and lashed upward. There was a sharp, resonant crack as the punch went home.

"That's the style, Danny!" Squires was yelling. "Send them in! Send them in!"

The voice of Squires raised a cold fury in him. He remembered in a flash the little roll of shabby dollar bills. So they were to cheat old Tom out of that! He was to go home to his wife and boy with eight thousand dollars, and Tom was to go home without his last fifteen! His left thudded home on the face, and his right thundered over on the temple like a trip hammer.

They were struggling in a clinch. The Swede was snarling in his ear:

"What's this? The double cross?"

Danny wanted to answer. He groped for words.

"No!"he gasped. "No! It's the square deal. That's what it is."

The referee wrenched them apart. The Swede was balancing himself on his toes and swaying his shoulders threateningly.

"All right, you imposter!" he shouted. "Just wait!"

Then it seemed to Doran as if great waves lifted him and smashed him up against the ropes. Giant drumsticks were beating a tattoo on his head and shoulders. He fought back gamely with right and left.

The end was near, he felt. All right, he would meet it as a man should. The thought of the boy at home ticked into his mind like a message. He had been wrong. The boy should fight his own battle. That was what he would have wanted himself. He would fight as his father was fighting now. He would win if he had the stamina and strength and skill; if he hadn't, he should lose like a man. There should be no shameful secret conferences behind locked doors, no passing of soiled money between furtive hands—a clean ring, and the prize to the winner; and might the best man win!

Rounds and rests were lost for him. He dimly heard the gong, and went to his corner, and rose when the gong crashed again. He was no longer conscious of the even voice of Dave, of the presence of Squires, of the panting, sweating seconds. He was at times sparring, at times leading snappy, smashing blows to head and jaw and body, at times clinching, at times reeling from the impact of jarring, deadening swings and hooks, and sending home counters like sword thrusts.

The house was too tense for shouting now. This was too great a fight to be true. Surely, they thought, no man could withstand those hurtling, cyclonic rushes of the giant Swede, with his arms swishing home like flails, and his great body behind them giving murderous force to every blow. And still there was the old champion crouching stealthily about the ring, his jaw and stomach well covered, his great, gnarled arms shooting out now and again like the paw of a cat and sending home those stinging, lightning punches that had made him so terrible in the old days. Neither of them could stand the pace long. Already the challenger's mouth was beginning to sag from the champion's flashing leads. And old Danny's ribs were angry and red from the crashing force of the kidney punch. There was a scarlet weal on his cheek bone where an old gash had opened, and his stomach and chest were purple from the Swede's short, infighting uppercuts.

Back in the hall the bookmakers were shouting in a frenzy. Doran heard them faintly, as through a wall :

"Even money! We'll give even money! We'll give even money!"

He felt a warm glow through him. He had been fighting, then, and fighting well. When he did go down, they couldn't blame him. He had done his best. He had played the game.

The seconds dashed water at him as he staggered to the corner. Things cleared as the sponge passed over his forehead. The air from the flapping towels gushed into his lungs as from a blast pipe. In the opposite corner he could see the Swede's seconds working like fiends. They were slapping and pummeling the challenger's legs. The Swede must be feeling the pace, too, he thought. That was all right.

"What's the round?" he asked.

"The twelfth," a second whispered.

Z.O.

He felt himself go taut like a rope. This was the round in which he was to have lain down. He felt a great impatience while he waited for the bell to ring. This was the round he would probably be knocked out in, but this was the round he must fight above all others. He waxed his shoes carefully on the resin board.

And then suddenly he was sparring, his eyes focused on the blazing grey eyes of the challenger. He forgot the brown gloves and the swinging arms and the pulsing, iron body. To keep his eyes on his man and to go down fighting, that was what he must do—to go down fighting, like the old heroes of the ring, as old John L. had gone down, and Peter Jackson, and the fighting "Fitz". One last rally, and then defeat! And to have played the game, the big game, a man's game!

He met the rush with a rain of jabs, and then the ropes cut into his back. He was being swung around and pushed mercilessly toward a corner. There was a jarring smash to his head. He shook it off like an insect and flailed back.

The house was on its feet. He could hear them shouting like the beating of great surf on rocks. The sound seemed to quiver and vibrate. The ring beneath his feet trembled like a springboard. He lashed out blindly again and again. He knew nothing but that he was fighting the last round of his last fight. His knees were sagging. Huge waves of crimson seemed to roll in, curl, and break before his eyes. His arms went out in great, titanic blows. There was a shock in his shoulders as his gloves struck home. The yelling of the audience crashed in his ears like volleys of thunder.

There was a heavy thud, and the ring seemed to rock beneath his feet. His right hand lashed through empty air. He caught the ropes, and staggered around again.

The referee was pushing him back.

"Stand away, Danny! Stand back! One! Two–"

Where was Nelson? He looked around stupidly. Why wasn't he fighting? What had happened? He caught sight of a huge, huddled figure lying crumpled on the canvas as through a haze of smoke. The thunderous shouting had ceased. In the dead silence he heard the voice of the referee count, like the slow ticking of a clock:

"Five ! Six ! Seven–"

He couldn't understand it. He should have been knocked out. And there was the Swede sprawling on the floor of the ring, and the count nearing the close.

"Nine! Ten! Out!"

Dave's arms were around him, he felt dully. They were leading him to his corner. The audience seemed to have suddenly become a horde of shrieking madmen. People were swarming into the ring and grasping his hand. He tried to pull himself together.

Now they were bathing his face; now they were taking his gloves off; helping him down from the ring and to the dressing room. They were in the dressing room now, Dave and Squires and he. They were cutting the bandages from his hands. He could hear Dave grunt as he bent over them. Squires was talking to himself quietly, in low, rambling tones.

L.O.

There were the voices of seconds in the corridor outside. They were raised for a moment in high-pitched argument :

"Well, I got the tip that Danny was going to lie down, I tell you!"

"For Heaven's sake, don't make a fool of yourself! Danny Doran lie down? Why, man, you're mad! You ought–"

The tension inside him seemed to snap like a string and to leave him weak and helpless. His head fell forward on his chest. There was a choke in his throat, and a warm trickle from his eyes that reached the cuts on his cheek bones and set them smarting furiously.

Dave looked up at him. "Ah, don't, Danny!" he said. "Ah, don't!" The choke became a sob. The warm trickle on his cheeks a stream. Dave began patting one shoulder, Squires the other.

"Ah, Danny, boy!" Dave was saying. "Ah, Danny!"

He couldn't stop the sobbing; he didn't want to. It seemed to him that all evening lean, sinewy fingers had been clutching his throat and were now loosing hold. He felt somehow that he was being relieved, that the tears running into the open gashes on his cheek bones were healing waters, and the patting of the trainer's hands the touch of a kindly physician.

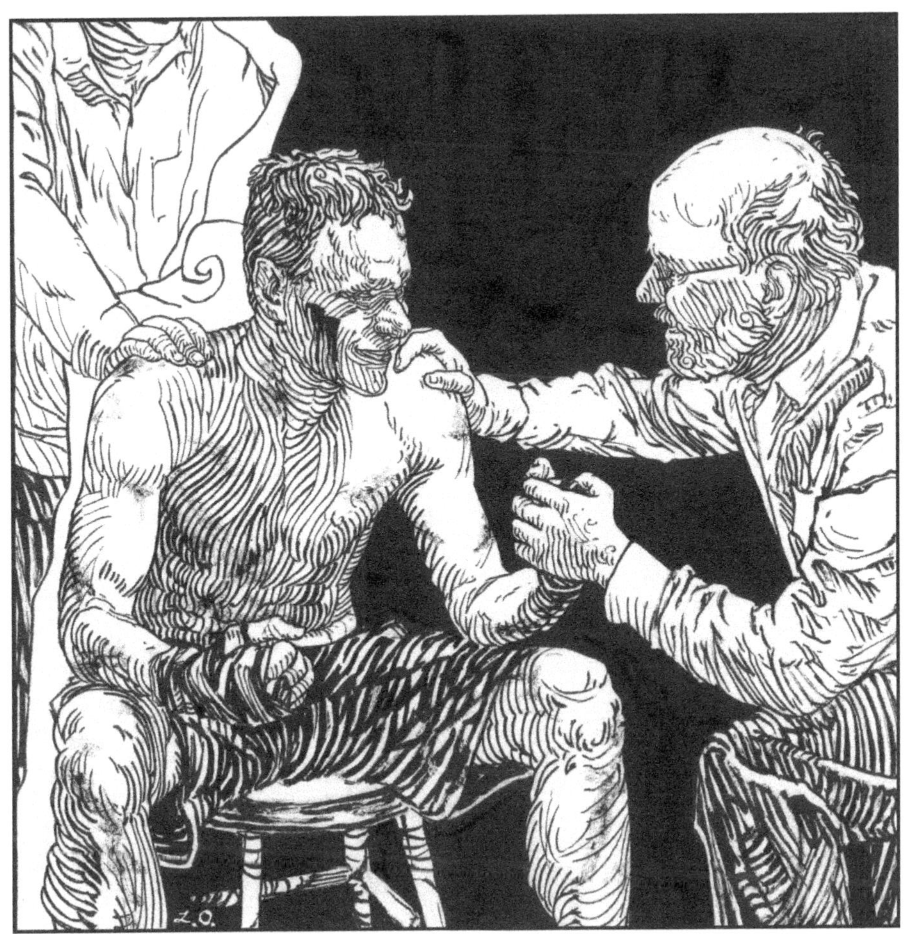

the end

DONN BYRNE

Donn Byrne (Brian Oswald Donn-Byrne) was born in 1889 during is Irish parent's business trip to New York City. Owing to this only omewhat unexpected happenstance, he lived in New York for the first ıree months of his life. In 1912 of his own volition he returned there › live and that's where he first discovered he could be—then showed e would be—a prolific and successful fiction writer. All the same, he prever regarded himself to be an Irishman from head to heart to heels, nd through loving and living life to the hilt, he always acted Irish. He 'as raised in County Armagh, a hilly region of northern Ireland. Then fter his second (but only willful) stint in America had completely layed out in 1922, he happily returned to Ireland to live, work, raise family and further his authorial career. Unfortunately, he died :agically in Ireland in 1927 when a faulty steering gear in his auto prced him off a cliff and into high tide of the bay below. He drowned t only thirty-eight years of age.

Donn Byrne always had a way with words and an abiding interest ı the entire lexicons of both English and Gaelic. As a young lad in :ounty Armagh, he always helped arrange the language festivals he von over and over again to the grumbling dismay of his competitors. Jevertheless, they couldn't help but like the boy for his singing, harm, nimble wit, self-assurance, friendliness, and readiness to talk to nyone about anything. And although relatively small in size as a boy, e was also gifted athletically. Eventually, as he advanced in age and ize, he won the lightweight boxing championship at Trinity College ı Dublin while studying romance languages and Irish literature, vinning, unsurprisingly, various prizes and scholarships in these ursuits as well.

The two illustrated boxing stories in this micro collection of two help emonstrate why Donn Byrne was able to succeed as an author. He rew upon his love of nature and a wide breadth of outdoor life (fishing, unting, horsemaship, etc.) and athletic activities, plus rambunctious social xperiences, to invent intimate stories. He then conveyed them in words e absorbed during his life-long fascination with language. But even hough all writers are into words and some undoubtedly could match)onn Byrne's intense relationship with language, few could match his bility to meld precise language with such a wide-ranging variety of life xperiences, for few if any had lived their lives as vigorously as he.

Liam O'Neil likes everything that comes with telling a good story. This could be a cascade of perfect words written to please the mind reading them. Or the pleasant smile of a cherished person they are read out loud to. Sometimes these words come with pictures and Liam makes these, for they believe this brings more delight to the discussion of minds and words. Liam's work is done almost completely traditionally, specializing in watercolor and pen and ink. They received a BFA in Illustration from the SCAD, and currently live in Saint Paul, MN. You can find more of their work at oneil-illustration.com and read some stories that they've written themselves (and made pictures for).

Jerome Tiller lives in Minneapolis, Minnesota. He is owner of ArtWrite Productions, a publishing company bent on making education and reading more pleasurable for youth. Adapted Classics, an imprint of ArtWrite Productions, uses fine-art illustrations to introduce classic stories to young readers. Learn more about Jerome and his company at: artwriteproductions.com and adaptedclassics.com

www.ingramcontent.com/pod-product-compliance
Lightning Source LLC
Chambersburg PA
CBHW040542170726
48295CB00012B/557
* 9 7 8 1 9 3 9 8 4 6 3 8 9 *